CW00420842

Anna Sky is a writer of mostly BDSM and spanking erotica. She lives in West Yorkshire with her partner Stephen, and their unruly hound. Having been an avid reader of erotica for years, she more recently started writing, and a whole world of naughty words and possibilities opened up. She's been published by Peaches Press and House of Erotica, and has been accepted for multiple upcoming anthology releases. Follow her on Twitter @iamannasky or find out more on her website at http://www.iamannasky.com

# Naughty Shorts

An Eclectic Mix of Erotica Short Stories

Anna Sky

CAS

ISBN: 1508521956
ISBN-13: 978-1508521952

# CONTENTS

# WHY I WROTE THIS BOOK

I love writing erotica, coming up with new ideas and playing with words. Over the past few years, I've gathered lots of short stories on my hard drive. Some have been published previously, either on my own erotica blog, or other erotica websites whereas other stories are brand spanking new, never having been seen before. Rather than let them gather cyberdust, I put this collection together so they could be unleashed on the world.

Enjoy!

# SOUNDS OF THE NIGHT

I sometimes lay awake at night, my brain alternating between the mundane and the insane but still preventing me from sleeping. I like to lie still and listen, there's nothing to listen to really and it calms me. There's the occasional bark of a dog, or the insistent hum of a car getting louder, then quietening as it passes. Most of all though, I listen to your breathing. I like hearing the regular ins and outs of your breath as you lay behind me, loosely moulded to my shape, one arms casually slung over my waist. Even in sleep you like to hang on to what's yours.

As I lay there last night, I felt your cock stir. You let out a small moan and pulled me closer to you, your cock now pressing insistently into the small of my back. As you rubbed yourself lewdly and unconsciously against me, you woke up. I heard your breathing change, felt your body tense, your hand reaching down to the protrusion between your thighs.

You assumed I was asleep and I did nothing to tell you otherwise, wondering what you were going to do. I felt the movement of your hand start slowly stroking your cock, your breath quickening slightly. Then you slipped your free arm underneath me, so you could pull me tightly to you. Your breath tickled against my ear, in and out, in and out as your hand slid up and down your erection in perfect synchronised timing. I imagined what it would look like, your hand firmly moving up and down the shaft. Your fingers would be gripping tightly, and you'd be pulling the foreskin back to exactly the right degree, letting your fingers and thumb catch the head slightly on each movement.

Your breathing was faster, more ragged and then you started whispering in my ear. Your words wrapped around me like a cocoon, arousing me and exciting me as I lay there, trying to keep my own breathing deep and constant, so as not to disturb our reverie. The more you spoke, the closer you came to orgasm. You whispered to me about spanking and seduction, intimate pleasures spiked with torments. I could tell you were close now, your whole body tensing, your sexual energy getting ready to spring forth.

Your hand pumped vigorously and your hips thrust into the movement for those final few strokes. I felt your hot ejaculate hit my back, my name floating on your breath as you relaxed back into that post-orgasmic state. I handed you the tissues and like a perfect gentleman, you carefully wiped my back. "How long were you awake?" you whispered to me, not wanting to intrude too far into the quiet of the moment. "What did you hear?"

"Everything," I quietly replied as lay there, once more listening to the sounds of the night.

# LADY GODIVA'S PUNISHMENT SPANKING

*Did you know that a cock-horse is a slang term for an adult's knee? I didn't and it got me thinking about what riding a cock-horse could be. Peeping Tom was allegedly blinded by spying upon Godiva, but in this tale I thought a blindfold may be better used...*

\*\*\*

Lady Godiva sat impatiently awaiting her 'package'. She was immaculately dressed, as was always the case, except for the recent incident which by now, the whole of England would surely know. Her slender ring-clad fingers tapped gently upon the desk in front of her, and as she moved her legs into a more comfortable position, the bells on her shoes, the latest fashion from London, gave off a light tinkling sound. Not long now...

There was a sudden and efficient knock at the door. A wry smile passed over Godiva's face as she called out to her manservant to open the door. In marched two of her guards; between them was dragged a man, well-dressed, blindfolded and obviously terrified.

"You may let him go." Godiva commanded, and the guards obliged, allowing their captive to fall to his knees.

"You may take off your blindfold now." Godiva's voice dropped to a lower pitch and she almost purred her instructions.

The man hastily scrabbled at the cloth that was tightly tied around his eyes, and ripped it away. He knelt on the floor, blinking into the sudden and harsh light, desperately trying to focus and find out what was happening. Godiva thought the look of shock on his face as he registered exactly where he was, would

3

stay in her mind for quite some time.

"So, Thomas. You disobeyed me." Godiva circled around her hapless prey, acting every inch the cold bitch. Her bells jangled musically as she walked, yet did nothing to break the tension.

Thomas blinked at her, not quite believing that his normally warm and friendly client could change so suddenly. He realised then just how angry she was. "Lady Godiva, please, accept my deepest apologies," he blustered remorsefully, not daring to meet her eye. "I truly didn't mean to look. I really didn't. It's just that I caught a glimpse as I closed the door and the sight of your perfect alabaster skin. I couldn't look away..."

"Enough!" snapped Godiva. "I really couldn't care less. My husband was going to tax every last damn one of you into the ground. I had to do something to help you. All I asked for was a little respect in return."

As she came to stand in front of him, she said only a little more softly, "whatever can I do with you Thomas? You're my best tailor, but right now, I need to teach you a lesson so I know that you respect me." As though finally making up her mind, Godiva snapped "Get up!"

Striding over to her high-backed chair she sat down, looking almost regal in her stature. Dismissing the guards with a wave of her hand, and instructing her manservant to wait outside and guard the door. She very intently and deliberately started stripping the jewellery from her fingers.

Thomas shifted uncomfortably from foot to foot, wondering what was to be his fate.

Planting her feet firmly on the ground and feeling her anger still bubbling inside, Godiva fixated her stare on Thomas. "Drop your trousers and get over my knee. Now!"

Not daring to hesitate, Thomas draped himself over Godiva's knees and steadied himself for what was to come.

Flexing her fingers, Godiva gently stroking his buttocks, covered by his loose undergarments, in order to find the shape and texture of her target. Anger at his impudence overflowed and she aimed the first hit perfectly at his quivering arse. Her hand stung with the magnitude of the contact, and she felt Thomas stiffen beneath her. She smacked him again and again, as hard as she could muster her strength for.

Exhaling hard enough to grunt and taking great gulps of air, she continued to spank him. She allowed all her anger, all her shame at what her husband had forced her into doing, to erupt as she continued to wallop her quarry. Beads of sweat formed on her upper lip and across her chest and a dull ache in her arm grew quickly more intense, but she didn't stop.

Her palm stung so much that it was almost numb but still her anger wouldn't dissipate. Smack, smack, smack. Thomas writhed around in discomfort and above the noise of her relentless admonishment she could hear him murmuring.

"Please, please ma'am." His words were barely recognisable sobs. "I'm so sorry Lady Godiva. Please have mercy upon me." It was a mantra of contrition. "I was unforgivably weak."

Something inside Godiva seemed to die down. The white-heat of her anger slowly ebbed and ignoring the twinges of pain, she gradually lessened the impact of her blows, until she stopped her punishment and felt able to speak.

"On your feet Thomas." she ordered, unsure of what to do next, or how she was going to look him in the eye the next time he came to measure her for one of his wonderful tailored creations.

"Yes ma'am." Thomas got to his feet, a model of penitence. Something in his tone made Godiva look towards him, and she almost gasped aloud. His cock was obviously engorged, the tip pushing almost painfully against his now-tight undergarments.

As he turned away to hastily pull on his trousers, she allowed herself a small smile. That was how she was going to be able to look him in the eye. He obviously just needed to be taken in hand, and what better way for her to blow off a little steam from time to time?

# ROOM 269

The hotel room was huge with a luxurious thick carpet that implied comfort was a necessity, not an option. Fashionable flock wallpaper and tasteful art adorned the walls, and peeping into the bathroom, Kerry smiled at the sight of the roll-top bath. She sighed with happiness; it was going to be a great weekend. "Jake baby, you chose well." The main room was dominated by a huge bed, made up with crisp white sheets and covered in cushions. Kerry laughed, threw down her bag and starfished herself right into the middle of it, knocking the cushions out of the way. "Hey, baby," she called, "come and join me."

She watched as Jake dropped their suitcase, and hurriedly emptied his pockets onto the desk. He crawled on to the bed and moved until he was on top of her, still on all fours. He lowered his mouth to hers, and kissed her deep and hard, enough that she moaned in pleasure, reaching up into him for more. Dropping his body to hers, Kerry thrust her hips up to meet his, happy to find his erection bearing down into her.

"You are a very bad influence," Jake whispered into her ear. His warm breath tickled her neck and he nibbled at her ear lobe. It was enough to send a little frisson of pain and pleasure shooting through Kerry's body.

"Oh yeah?" she replied, snaking her hands round to Jake's bottom. She tucked her hands into his jeans pockets and playfully squeezed his buttocks through the thin fabric. "What are you going to do about it?"

"Hmm." Jake reached round and extracted one of her hands, pinning her wrist down to the bed, above her head. He did the same with the other, and Kerry squirmed beneath him. "Perhaps you need punishing young lady, for being so wanton with your desires." He kissed down her neck with big mouthing movements he knew would turn her on.

Kerry laughed. "Wanton with my desires? Have you just jumped from a Victorian period drama? And besides, good Sir, you ain't seen nothing yet!" She pushed her hips up into Jake, enjoying the increased pressure between her thighs. The mild teasing so far had set off the familiar throb and she knew it could only lead to one thing. How long it would take depended on how Jake was feeling. Would he tease and torment her until she begged him to let her come, or would he be in the mood to take her hard and fast, ensuring her pleasure as well as his own?

Pinning her wrists with one hand, Jake slid his other hand down Kerry's body. She was held fast, and let herself relax. Whatever he did next, was totally out of her control and in his hands. She might as well enjoy it, rather than trying to fight back or take control herself. Neither of them enjoyed it as much as when she let Jake take the lead.

Jake stroked his hand down her face, trailing his fingers over her cheek and down her jawline. His thumb brushed over her lips and she automatically opened her mouth slightly, allowing him access. He let his hand slide to lightly hold against her throat and brought his mouth to hers again, pressing his lips hard against her own, forcing her mouth open wider as his tongue pushed in.

Kerry was lost in a sea of emotion. He knew how to turn her on, make her want, no, need him, so badly. When they played like this, her entire world shrunk to being just them. The sensitive pressure of his hand on her neck alone was enough to send her in to a different headspace but with his cock nestling into the apex of her thighs and him kissing her so hard she could barely breathe, she thought she was going to explode from pleasure. And he had barely begun his assault on her body.

He lifted away slightly and worked his hand under her vest-top to her bra. Pulling the cups down, he lifted her breasts out and squeezed and kneaded each one in turn. Kerry couldn't help herself and whimpered in pure pleasure. Jake grinned. "I'm glad you're enjoying yourself, you're going to be moaning and whimpering for a while yet though."

He took one of her nipples and rolled it between his forefinger and thumb, gradually increasing the tightness of his grip. It was beautifully painful, with shots of pleasure coursing through her body, all adding to the pressure that was building in her sex as Jake slowly led her inexorably closer to an explosive climax.

Kerry tried pushing her hips up again and he laughed, moving himself away much to her frustration. "Oh no," he said. "Only good girls get orgasms, and we've already established that you're not one of those." She moaned in frustration at his words. He was going to make her work so hard for the relief she so desperately craved, it was going to be almost painful.

Jake rolled onto his side, still holding her wrists. He carefully unbuttoned her jeans, and worked them down her thighs. "Why don't you kick them off?" he suggested, although she knew it wasn't really a question. She worked her feet out of her jeans and heard them fall to the floor. Jake's hand slid up and down her upper legs, pinching and rolling the flesh on her inner thighs. She tried pressing her legs together; the sensations were almost overwhelming.

She was rewarded with a short sharp tap on the

inside of her thigh, before Jake roughly pushed her legs apart. "Did I tell you to do that?" he asked, his voice sounding a little sterner.

"No, Jake," she whispered, another shot of lust coursing through her veins.

"That's better." Jake continued tormenting her inner thighs. He stopped and grinned. "I think I should spank you." He released her wrists. "Get up!"

Kerry stood up, feeling suddenly vulnerable. Jake sat on the edge of the bed, knees slightly apart and pulled her over his knee. She wriggled into a better position, trying to balance herself whilst at the same time ensure she were able to press her throbbing clitoris down onto Jake's knee or thigh. He waited until she finished before moving her again, a silent warning that he was in charge.

She groaned inwardly. Of course it had been a long shot, but it had been worth trying anyway, just in case. Jake's hand swept over her bottom, squeezing each buttock a few times to prime her flesh. He landed the first blow solidly on her left buttock, causing her to move forward slightly to lessen the impact.

"Oh, Kerry," Jake admonished. "You know you're supposed to stay still!" He pulled her arms into the small of her back, and held in place by her wrists. She groaned again, he was in one of those moods and was determined not to give her the tiniest bit of slack. Held firmly in place, Kerry waited for the next blow to land. He went for exactly the same spot as before, causing her to suck her breath in through her teeth. If she couldn't absorb the pain physically, she would have to focus on her breathing and let the spanking sensations wash over her.

Jake stopped for a moment, running his hand over her bottom and sliding his hand between her legs. He ran his fingers lightly over the fabric of her panties, pulling back as Kerry tried pushing down onto his hand. It was added torture, the slightest touch of his fingers through the thin cotton and her total inability to move. He circled over her clitoris a few times before pinching it gently. She mewled, desperate for him to continue, to let her come but she knew that he would make her wait. He pulled her panties down and Kerry felt the air on her wet sex. She moaned, helpless under Jake's control.

Jake continued to spank, covering her now-naked bottom in bright red marks. He built up a rhythm, a fairly fast-paced hard wallop that made her take big, deep breaths, exhaling on the strikes to cope with the pain. It came over her in waves, the initial pain of the strike followed by a warm glow that rippled out from the impact point. All her nerve endings seemed to be on fire, and she was desperate for orgasmic release. Jake did such a good job of winding her up, all the things he so deliberately did, knowing the exact effect his actions had on her.

He finished with a crescendo of hard hits, in the same spot, one set on each side. Kerry managed a wry grin – he was landing them on her 'sit spot' and knew that every time she sat down for the next day or two, she'd feel the results of his handiwork.

"Stand up," Jake ordered, releasing her wrists. Kerry did as he said, moving her arms to get her circulation moving. "Mmm," he said, looking her up and down appreciatively. He backed her onto the bed, until he was poised on top of her again. "I want to fuck you now. Give you that release that you've been so desperate for. But only if you ask me nicely enough. What do you say?"

"Thank you Jake," Kerry's face showed her relief. "Please, please fuck me. Please let me come."

"Is that all you've got?" He ran his index finger gently along her cleft, dipping two fingers in suddenly, coating them in her juices. "I think you can do better than that." He traced the same fingers over her lips and pushed them into her mouth.

Kerry was desperate; her tangy scent, full of musk and Jake's promises drove her mad with desire. "Please, Jake. Please fuck me, let me come." She exhaled with relief as he stood up and stripped off; the sight of his naked body never failed to excite her and right now, she knew he wanted the same thing as her, a mind-blowing fuck. He lay back down on the bed next to her and his cock caught against her thigh taunting her along with his words.

"That's better," he grinned. "But you have to call out my name as you come. I want to hear you." He deftly rolled a condom on and manoeuvring himself on top, pushed himself between her thighs. Kerry was slick with need after all his ministrations, and he slid in with no further lubrication needed.

He eased in and out excruciatingly slowly. Kerry pushed upwards to persuade him to push in deeper to no avail. She reached round and grabbed at his bottom and thighs to pull him closer but Jake was having none of it, exercising a level of self-control that she found almost super-human. He gently bit at her jawline and neck, fondled her breasts and continued to tease her with his cock, pushing in slowly and rolling his weight across her clitoris before pulling out again, leaving her hungry for more.

Jake repeated the process over and over, and Kerry felt herself approaching climax, the tension was almost unbearable. Her head spun as she felt him press hard against her, the sensation of him grabbing and squeezing her breasts and her nipples hard enough to make her gasp, the sharp nip of his teeth against her neck; she span out of control.

Waves of pleasure crashed into each other and washed over her and she felt herself pulsing hard around his cock. The tension in her whole body gradually eased as she relaxed, not realising until then how tightly wound up she'd been. A voice echoed in her ears and with a start, Kerry realised it was her own, calling out Jake's name, as he'd instructed, over and over.

As she came back down, Jake upped the tempo of his thrusting, pulling in and out in a fast, thrusting motion. She pulled him closer, a trick she knew he liked. Wrapping her legs around his, she squeezed his buttocks with one hand, her other arm cradling the back of his neck. Jake moaned as she kissed his shoulders and chest, and moments later collapsed on top of her, a sheen of sweat sticking their bodies together as he came.

Kerry smiled, it was going to be a great weekend away.

# SPACE

I drifted weightlessly from my cabin, still childish enough to enjoy the zero gravity. Propelling myself along the wall, I entered the main deck where Tom was frowning at a control panel.

"Hey!" I greeted him, "How's it hanging?"

"Oh hi Kat." Tom grinned ruefully at my joke. The same one I asked every time I saw him. It was all part of the big flirt. There was nothing in the rules to say that we couldn't get down and dirty, well dirty at least as there's no such thing as down, 200 miles above the Earth with no gravity. However, I didn't think any relationship would be met with ecstatic applause, as our station was very small and we still had another few months on board before the relief crew arrived.

"I'm just finishing off these notes, then do you fancy grabbing a bite to eat?" Tom grinned at me again.

"Okay," I agreed, "Chinese or Indian?" I grinned back at him, knowing that neither of these were on the menu.

Tom flung his pen at me and it spun in graceful arcs, hitting the console behind me, narrowly missing my ear. It was immediately followed by a persistent bleeping sound. I grimaced and turned round to see what the problem was.

Nothing appeared to be amiss and I hit the console's reset button, stopping the noise when suddenly I felt Tom's body press up against mine, pushing me into the panel.

He is 6'2" to my 5'5" and I knew it was his chest pushing against the back of my head, his legs and torso pushing into me. After so many months alone, first in the training stages and then in space itself, to feel another human, this real human of flesh and bone pushed into me was amazing. I gasped with pleasure, relief and so many other mixed emotions.

"Kat," he throatily whispered my name. "Oh Kat." His hot breath brushed across my neck and I thought I could hear my own feelings reflected in his voice. The longing, the anguish and dammit, the loneliness. I'd fancied Tom ever since I first clapped eyes on him in training and we became steadfast friends. I never wanted to ruin that, so always held back, us flirting in ever decreasing circles around each other, neither one of us breaking, or perhaps more likely, not daring to make that first move.

I couldn't bring myself to say anything, hardly daring to breathe, full of hope and desire, and Tom thought he got it wrong, backing off quickly. "Oh, Kat, I'm sorry, I fucked up. Please..." and with that he was gone from the deck, pulling himself along on the hand rails to speed his flight.

Shit, what was I supposed to do now? I did the only thing I thought possible and followed him. Tom was wedged in his bunk, head in his hands. I sat next to him, hooking myself in, and took his hands in my own.

"You didn't fuck up, Tom. I just didn't know what to say or do. I want this as much as you do, but I was scared."

"Shit, Kat, you're just saying that now." Tom looked so dejected and in that instant, all I wanted to do was hold him, kiss him, stroke his hair, tell him it was okay. I reached out to him and taking his jaw with my fingertips, turned his head to face me and slid my hand so it was cradling his cheek.

I kissed him gently on the lips and he tasted of sweat, summer evenings playing out in the fields, of desire, instinct and incarceration on this little space station. My insides turned to pools of jelly, and hoping beyond hope, I wanted, no needed, him to reciprocate.

And reciprocate he did. With a sudden and animal ferocity, he gripped my face in his hands, pushing his lips down on to mine, seeming to search out my soul with his tongue.

Suddenly we were off our feet. Caught up in our lust, we'd momentarily forgotten to account for the lack of gravity and our movements had engineered us out of the bunk. We broke off from our kiss to laugh at what happened. The sheer joy of floating unexpectedly combined with the physical contact and the promise of release from all that pent-up desire and longing was heady.

Tom pushed off the bunk pressing his body against mine and I let his momentum take us backwards until he was pinning me against the wall. Of course, I could have pushed him off with my little finger, but I didn't want to. I wanted these moments to last. I felt his body press against me, his muscles and sinews primed. I felt his flat muscular stomach push against mine, his long sleek legs levering him into me, and oh joy, his big, hard cock nestling insistently between us.

Tom held us in place as I slid my hands up his t-shirt and he gasped. I continued to explore his upper body with my hands, wanting to touch every inch of him, drinking him in via my fingertips. He was an amazing specimen of a man, as you'd expect from all the years of training we'd undergone. But even so, his muscular physique, the thought of the power in those limbs took me by surprise and excited me beyond measure.

His lips were in my hair, kissing down to my face,

his teeth nipping at my jawline. It's like he couldn't get enough of my either. His hands started to roam, hesitantly at first as they encircled my waist, then more confidently as he heard a moan escape my lips.

We floated into the middle of the cabin and his strong hands manipulated my body with ease, pulling me up so our eyes met. He brought his lips back to meet mine, crushing them with an intensity that I'd never felt before. He held me in place and kissed, and kissed, and kissed. I felt myself getting so wet for him, so turned on that I'm sure he could have smelt that heady hormonal scent in the air.

I started working his t-shirt off, breaking only from our kiss to hastily pull it over his head. Tom did the same with me and we continued by taking off our station-issued jogging pants. I was floating, literally and metaphorically, in just my underwear and in his hands. And oh, he looked incredible, sleek, toned and muscular in just his tight boxers. His cock was straining hard at the fabric, desperate for release and relief.

"Damn Kat," he breathed at me, "you're so hot. I want you, I've always wanted you." And with that, I was back tightly in his arms, my body moulding itself to his every contour. He pushed me outwards and away from him as he lowered his lips to the centre of my collar bone and slowly moved his lips and tongue down my chest. I moaned, I was on fire. Every single nerve ending he touched connected through to the core of me, building to an insistent throb centring on my clitoris. His hands undid my bra and worked my breasts free and I was silently grateful for no gravity, as they stood pert and firm off my chest.

Tom circled first one nipple then the other, with his finger then with his tongue. He licked and sucked and grazed them with his teeth until I thought I was going to orgasm from that alone. He continued to play with my breasts and nipples with his fingers as his lips kept travelling down my torso. He glanced up at me, meeting my eye momentarily as if to reassure himself that this was real and not just another frustrating dream, before grazing his teeth over my white cotton panties. I felt that I was going to explode, the tightness of the fabric pressing against my mons and his hot breath winding me up to fever pitch.

Pulling himself back up, he pressed himself against me, propelling us both back into the cabin wall. "Stay there," he whispered huskily and spun round, searching for something amongst his possessions. Turning round again, I saw he had a small foil packet and I laughed. I guess some things from years of training never leave you. Be prepared for any eventuality!

With one easy movement, Tom had slipped on the condom and was out of his pants. "So, is this what you want Kat?" he whispered at me, gently rubbing his cock against the front of my panties. I couldn't believe it, here we were, finally daring to get it on and he was teasing me like this?!

"Yes!" I whispered breathily, "I want you Tom; I've wanted you for so long. I want to feel your cock inside me, feel our bodies intertwined..." As I confessed my innermost secrets, he slipped my panties off and I tailed off, hardly daring to breathe, wanting what was happening so damn much. Tom slid two fingers tentatively down between my legs, pushing my lips apart and exposing my frankly hot, and very wet pussy to the cooler air of the cabin. His fingers slipped in and out of me, again and again as his thumb circled insistently on my clitoris.

From not breathing at all, my breaths were now

hot and ragged, and I desperately tried to push back to meet Tom's hand. It was impossible though with the lack of gravity and my frustration grew by the second. All those months of no sexual contact and in just a few minutes, Tom had built up my tension so I was ready to burst.

Realising my intentions, he took his hand away and running his fingers over his lips, he licked them. "You taste so sweet, Kat. I want you now." He pushed his fingers into my mouth, making me taste my wanton desire, and using his handhold to keep us in position, buried his cock inside me. I gasped at the fullness, glad that my lust had made me so wet, as his large girth pressed insistently further into me.

Holding me so tight round my waist, Tom pushed up and into me and we took off. I positioned my arms over his shoulders and around his neck and pushing down on my forearms managed to create some movement. I wrapped my legs around his hips and in this way, we bounced around the cabin, free floating and fucking madly.

Every time Tom pushed back into me, I felt my orgasm build. My head was spinning and I wanted to explode. "Come for me Kat," Tom cajoled, his rough breath in my ear. "Oh Tom, oh Tom, oh Tom" it was all I could manage, all that build up, all that tension, coming down to a simple act of pleasure, the pressure of his cock in just the right place.

And then I was riding the waves of orgasm, hit after hit of euphoria, I thought it was never going to end. I felt Tom give a couple of last thrusts, feeling him clench and relax as his orgasm hit too. We ended up a tangled mess of limbs wedged back in the bunk, my head spinning, my body limp. Tom kissed my neck and shoulders, bringing his face up to meet mine. "Oh Kat," he whispered, stroking my hair back off my face "I'm not letting you go."

I nestled back satisfied into his arms almost purring with post-orgasmic pleasure. It wasn't going to be such a long few months left on the station after all. "So," I grinned at him, "Chinese or Indian for dinner?"

# MEMORIES OF A SPANKING

I look in the mirror, with fascination at the light bruises on my bottom. I finger them lightly, running my fingertips over the imprint of your fingertips, and remember with a smile how they'd got there.

We'd been play fighting the night before, me straddled over you on the bed, tickling you whilst you were telling me to stop. I didn't of course, so you flipped us over, your body pinning mine to the bed, your hands stretching my wrists above my head.

"You'd best stop that," you growled at me, "or you'll face the consequences young lady."

I laughed at you, and tried to kiss you, but you moved away from me to tease me. I pressed my body up to yours to try and reach you, feeling the contours of your chest press against my breasts.

"Oh, what consequences?" I pouted at you, moving in again for a kiss and failing.

"I don't know," you seem to ponder for a second or two and your eyes light up. "Perhaps I'll put you over my knee and spank you!"

"Yeah, right!" My disbelief at your words shot right out of my mouth. How ridiculous, of course you weren't going to spank me!

"Don't push me," you growled, your voice suddenly dark and slightly menacing. You ran one of your hands down my torso, on that edge where our bodies met, stopping to slide your fingers under my bottom and give it a quick, hard squeeze. A shiver ran down my spine.

"Ow, what did you do that for?" I tried to struggle under you, as amusement played in my voice. It didn't hurt of course, but I thought we were still playing. The idea of a spanking started growing in my mind. Half of me loved the idea, wanted to know what it would feel like, but the other half of me firmly decided that I didn't want the pain or humiliation of having you bring your hand down on my buttocks, like I were a small child punished for being naughty.. One of my hands came free of yours and before I knew what I was doing, I seemed to be goading you into doing exactly what you'd threatened.

"I warned you!" You stood up quickly, pulling me with you, and sat back down on the bed, your knees slightly parted and your feet flat on the floor. All the while you'd had hold of my wrists, and when you were done, you pulled me back over your knee!

"Wh..what do you think you're doing?" I was outraged, I never thought you'd actually do this, and now it was happening, I was even surer I wasn't going to like it.

"Teaching you the consequences of not listening to me young lady," you calmly replied, bringing your hand down in a light swat first on my right cheek and then my left, and then again.

It didn't hurt, so I thought I was going to get away with it. Little did I know that my arrogance was going to be my downfall. I writhed under your touch, desperately trying to work out what my next move was.

"If you stop struggling, it won't be as bad." I could hear the amusement in your voice, you willing me to misbehave.

And of course, I defiantly played right into your hands, literally. You scooped my wrists together behind me, and held them in the small of my back, partly steadying me, partly pinning me. You spread your knees slightly wider to counterbalance my shift in weight and that's when the spanking really started.

Your light taps turned into heavier blows,

alternating between my cheeks, spank, spank, spank, getting faster and in a definite rhythm. I couldn't wriggle, couldn't get away from the increasing pain in my bottom. You paused for a few seconds, and I was idly wondering how red my posterior was when I felt you lift up my skirt and pull down my panties. I felt my face go red, embarrassed at what you were doing, but didn't have time to complain as your next volley of blows started.

You spanked me all over my behind from the tops of my buttocks down to where they met my thighs, and after the first few minutes of pain, I realised that it didn't hurt any more. Instead of the sting of your hand meeting my skin, I could feel a sensual warmth spreading through me from that contact point, making my clit tingle, my nipples harden and a growing yearning for you deep inside me.

The closer towards the middle of my bottom that you spanked, the more I whimpered in pleasure, feeling the aftershocks directly in my now-wet pussy. I realised that I was trying to raise my buttocks up to meet your hand, and you knew it too. You chuckled at me. "Naughty girl, I think that's enough punishment for tonight."

You helped me back onto my feet and I fell into you, your arms encircling me, your mouth pressed into mine. I knew then that I'd always find a way to misbehave for you; always now want you to put me over your knee and spank me like the naughty girl you'd just awakened.

# COCK TEASE

Be careful what you wish for, or at least be specific about it. Three days ago I woke groggily to the smell of anaesthetic; my head pounded and I felt heavy, displaced. I didn't dare open my eyes. Reaching out with dull, aching fingers that were mine, but not mine, I felt crisp sheets. A few inches more and I hit cold metal. Bars? I thought, No, cot sides!

The hairs on the back of my neck prickled. I wasn't alone in this room. Opening my eyes slowly, I groaned at the light, squinting into the brightness and let things slowly come into focus. It was like looking out through a stranger's face. The world was different. I was me, with my memories, but this body? It was big, heavy, not how I remembered myself.

"How are you feeling?" I heard a mysterious voice, silken tones bringing me back to full consciousness. I slowly swivelled my head around to look at its owner. There she was, Lucy, I remembered her name. She looked exquisite, dressed all in black, everything showing a figure to die for. Long sleeved, high neck lace blouse. Under-bust leather corset, laced to show her hourglass figure to perfection. Tight pencil skirt...I felt my cock twitch at the sight of her.

My cock twitch?! I felt nauseated.

"Hold on," Lucy rose from her chair and passed me a bucket. "They warned you, remember?" As I heaved into it, memories flooded back, faster and faster. Signing the paperwork for a new experimental procedure, the counselling, the conversation that kicked it all off – a drunken admission of cock envy. And oh! That was it, the missing piece of the puzzle. An agreement with Lucy, Mistress; she would pay for my mind to be implanted into a male body and I would be her slave, my body was now her body. A shudder ran through me, the enormity of what I had done, hit me. I heaved into the bucket again.

Mistress was gentle to me for the first couple of weeks, easing me slowly into my new body. Gone were my swinging hips and my full breasts. In their place I had muscular thighs, and a broad chest with a smattering of hair. The hair on my head was short; I enjoyed quick showers and felt only relief that I didn't have to worry about hair and make-up ever again. Once used to my limbs, I was stronger, faster and relished being the new me. In those first few weeks, Mistress helped me explore my new sexuality too.

On the first morning, we found my nipples were sensitive. "Perfect for clamps," she giggled gleefully, tying me down and finding all my weak spots. Over time, she found my ticklish places, sensitive areas that she would drag her nails over and then swat with her fingertips until I couldn't take any more. I never could escape her though; she tied me down too tightly. Most importantly to us both she spent hours teasing my cock. I revelled in my new-found symbol of masculinity. The feel of her hands or her mouth on it turned me into a quivering wreck. I would do anything for this woman, my mistress, and she knew it.

The day she let me fuck her was magnificent. She'd teased me for some time, keeping me on the edge, begging and desperate. I felt the now-familiar tightening in my balls and abdomen over and over, but she wouldn't let me come, despite my pleading. To silence me, she thrust my head between her legs and let me swirl and lick, suck and lave, until her head tipped back, her throat exposed and she floated into blissful yet violent peaks of orgasm. She found it a distinct advantage that I'd once been female; whenever we'd finished one of our sessions, she would stroke my hair and call me the most considerate male lover she'd ever had.

That day, once I'd made her come to her satisfaction, Mistress rolled on to her back and spread her legs apart for me. My cock, already hard, felt like it was about to explode. I nudged it into her folds, slick and warm, and slowly pushed inside her. I let her juices coat me, lubricating my shaft as I slid in and out, feeling her squeeze around me until I came hard and fast. It felt so sensitive, so exquisite, so damn perfect. I cried.

Those first few weeks were a grace period, I see that now. Mistress was kind and loving, and gave me only a few rules to abide by. She liked me to wear a collar, a symbol of her ownership. I was proud when she locked it on to me, and regularly polished the leather and chrome. At mealtimes, she asked that I wait until she'd had the first bite; only then was I allowed to eat, and she dictated small details such as my bedtime. Perhaps I took my new life for granted, as I violated her last rule, no touching myself without her express permission.

I couldn't help it; I'd wanted a cock all my life, and now I had one. The feel of it swelling, the chafing of the head against my jeans was a delicious agony and one morning, it was one that I just couldn't bear. Without thinking of what I was doing, I started playing, letting my hand squeeze up and down the shaft, catching the tip with a delicious jolt. I was so close, oh so close, when I realised Mistress was watching me, a half-grin on her face, but her eyes glinting dangerously.

"You'd best stop doing that right now." The cold edge in her voice, and my fear that I'd disappointed her, cut me to the core.

Mistress was fair to me. I broke her rule, so until I could be trusted, she would be in charge of my cock. She locked it into a chastity cage. I nearly wept as she manipulated the cold steel over my testicles. The key went on a short chain around her neck; I saw it every time I looked at reminder of my failure. And once she had me by my balls, she spanked me.

Over her knee I stayed, helpless against her punishment and emasculated by the device, until she'd finished admonishing me. My buttocks stung for hours after; the mosaic of bruises became a second, more temporary reminder of my crime, although they took days to fade.

I once wished to have a cock. That was a mistake. I should have wished to have one that I could play with whenever I liked.

# INNOCENCE

Sarah smiled. She thought she might have just made a sale. The young couple she was showing round the Georgian town house seemed delighted with the property.

The house itself was on three floors, nestled into a row of similar properties, all sharing an imposing façade. The couple had initially been very quiet when she had led them in through the front door but they'd rapidly grown more animated as they'd seen how their existing life could fit into this possible new one. They were enamoured by the period features – half-hidden little alcoves, original fire surrounds, high ceilings and all the traditional details that were expected in a house of that age.

Mr Felling, or George, as he'd told Sarah to call him loved the solid walls between them and next door. "Not like our place in London, Suze," he'd laughed as he knocked firmly on the dining room wall, separating them from their potential neighbours. "We'll be able to crank up the volume and no-one will hear a thing!" Sarah smiled politely and idly wondered what sort of hi-fi system he had.

Continuing on, Sarah showed them the beautiful kitchen, complete with a separate island, marble worktops and plenty of seating space. The sitting room was next followed by the downstairs cloakroom. Sarah learnt that George and Suzie both worked in high-flying banking jobs in London and were looking to move to somewhere, still with the amenities of a city but with a slightly slower pace of life.

"Besides," Suzie added, "most of our friends live closer to here anyway." She flashed George a smile, with mischief in her eyes and he smiled back. Sarah led the couple up the first flight of stairs and turned to a door. "This is what the current owners are using for a study," she explained, moving into the room to allow George and Suzie to see the room, complete with its floor to ceiling bookcases.

George walked behind the desk, looking around. "Perfect for my big old desk, don't you think, Suze?" He was looking at his wife over the top of his glasses in a mock headmasterly-way, and Suzie giggled, agreeing with him. Sarah was accustomed to private jokes and had long ago learnt to be discreet and not to ask questions so she smiled and continued her tour.

The family bathroom was next followed by two small bedrooms that Suzie declared were perfect for guests, "or family," she added quickly. The final room on that floor was slightly larger. "I can't get over the size of the rooms, George. You actually could swing a cat in here. Not like at home..!"

George looked around appraisingly. "This could make a lovely playroom," he concluded. "A big toy box in the corner, all those blank walls for us to fill. Yes," he paused, "yes, we could really make this home ours."

Again Sarah smiled. George had just used the word "home." She was sure the couple would put in an offer. And it was lovely that he was thinking about a playroom for the children they were so obviously planning.

"I'll show you the final floor," she said, leading them up the next flight of stairs. Suzie gasped at the size of the master bedroom, currently complete with an imposing four-poster bed yet with more than ample room for a dressing table and a chaise longue.

"George..," Suzie began, "Do you think I could have

my hanging chair in here?"

George laughed, "You and that bloody chair! Yes, I'm sure there'll be a beam up there somewhere that we can attach your chair to. Then you can sit and swing and read your book, or do whatever you want in it!" Suzie beamed and clapped her hands together girlishly.

"We have a walk in wardrobe here..." Sarah opened the door to yet another huge space. It was truly impressive with mirrors running full-length down the walls, and hanging rails at varying different heights. Suzie gripped George's hand tightly. "It's perfect!" she exclaimed, whilst staring in wonder.

"I'll leave you to look at this and the ensuite bathroom." Sarah decided to give the couple some space to make their decision. "I'll be downstairs in the kitchen if you have any questions..."

***

A few months later, after the sale had gone through successfully, Sarah was at her desk when she realised that Jeannie, one of her colleagues had sidled over.

"Hey Sarah," Jeannie started, "you sold the property on Morsten Street, didn't you?"

"Yeah, I did," Sarah frowned, "why are you asking?"

"What were the buyers like?" Jeannie was leaning forwards now, as though Sarah were about to unlock some secret.

"The Fellings? Oh, lovely." Sarah replied. "They wanted a family home. They were planning playrooms and all sorts when I showed them round."

Jeannie laughed, "Yeah, playroom...There's rumours you know. About parties. You know the sort. Leather and whips. Kinky parties." At the word kinky, Jeannie's voice had dropped to a whisper.

Sarah looked at Jeannie. "No, really? Surely not!" She gasped as the penny dropped… "oh!".

Sarah's cheeks flushed red as memories of showing the couple round came flooding back. The big desk in the study, where George reminded her of a headteacher? The playroom, oh no! That toy box wasn't for children's toys was it? And they never did say what they wanted to fill the walls with!

Visions of slaves being flogged whilst tied to those walls sprang to mind. They even mentioned about room to swing a cat! And of course, the Fellings were quite happy that the house had natural sound-proofing weren't they? They weren't thinking about a stereo, more about the screams!

What was that about a hanging swing..? Oh! A different kind of swing than Sarah had had in mind. And the walk-in wardrobe? Visions of all sorts of kink started filling her head as she remembered the full walls of mirrors, and all those fixed rails.

Sarah groaned, how could she have been so naïve?

# FIRST SPANKING

The first time Matt spanked me, it nearly ended our relationship. I always knew I was kinky but until I met him, my deeper desires had never been explored. I loved being with him - we made each other laugh, shared a love of red wine, and he was great in bed too. He understood that my kink was more than just a pair of fluffy handcuffs. As our relationship developed, so did our exploration of our fantasies.

Although gentle to start with, we both became more confident in what we did and I would find myself in more intensive submissive situations. Like the time he pushed me to my knees, fastened my arms behind my back, and fisted his hands into my hair to lever his cock deeper into my mouth. He loved being in control and every time he treated me like this a thrill ran through me. I felt objectified, used, ecstatic.

Or when he tied me down, and fulfilled my desires to submit, both physically and mentally. Each time, my limbs were stretched tightly towards a corner of the bed, with no chance of escape. He slipped a blindfold on me, and I felt his hot breath tickling my ear as he whispered that I must keep still and trust him. He teased and probed until I was breathless, dizzy with lust and desperate for climax. Matt consistently knew how to get my body to respond; he squeezed and stroked, nipped and licked, and laughed at my indignant and futile attempts to wriggle away from his ministrations.

He struggled too though, with some things. I wanted to experience a combination of pain and pleasure. Deep in my psyche, I knew that's what I needed. But he didn't want to hurt me, even consensually. Sure, he would occasionally tweak my nipples or gently pinch my inner thighs, but what I really wanted him to do was pull me down across his knee and spank me hard.

I think I pestered him for long enough. One night, he told me to go and wait for him in the bedroom. This was his way of telling me to get undressed and kneel on the floor facing away from the door, knees apart and hands clasped behind my back. He never left me for long in my submissive pose, just enough time for me to slip into a different head space.

Matt walked into the room that fateful night, barefoot so I could barely hear him move. Usually I would hear him open our toy box, and try to guess what he was retrieving. Tonight, he simply sat on the edge of the bed.

"Come here." He commanded, a confident edge of dominance in his voice. I stood and walked to him, head down, hands behind my back. I was the model of a good submissive, exactly the way he liked me to behave. "It's time," he said and roughly pulled me down over his knee. A deep and visceral shiver ran through me; I felt that all the dots were being connected at last.

Matt spent a few moments moving me into place. At the time I thought it was part of the psychological warfare he so loved inflicting. Looking back, I realise it was simply nerves. He pulled my legs apart, moving my feet into a position that made my balance harder to maintain. Letting his hand slide between my legs, he pushed two fingers inside me and found me wet and ready for him. He chuckled, a low rumble that reverberated through my torso where our flesh touched. He moved my hands too, shoulder-width apart. I felt vulnerable and excited, uncomfortably held in place on Matt's wide thighs. Goosebumps formed on my arms and I pressed my body down into him, trying to suck the warmth from his skin and calm my wildly beating heart.

Once satisfied, Matt massaged my buttocks, kneading the flesh. I moaned, pushing up into his hands; the feel of them grabbing me repeatedly was bliss. But I wanted and was desperate for more. When he finally moved one hand into the small of my back I relaxed, breathing deeply and waited for his first strike. When it came though, it was a half-hearted blow, full of power and promise yet totally failing to deliver. I waited for more, wondering whether it was all part of him teasing me, or a slow warm up perhaps.

"Get up." His voice was unsteady. I stood, and without another word, Matt strode out of the room. I lay down on the bed and wrapped myself tightly in the duvet, feeling vulnerable and confused.

\*\*\*

"Hey." Matt was quiet as he lay down next to me, pulling me towards him. He tightly enveloped me in his arms, my body still encased in the duvet.

"What happened?" I asked, unsure of whether I wanted the answer or whether I just needed to fill the silence.

With his free hand, Matt stroked my hair away from my face and twisted his fingers into its length. He always played with my hair when he was nervous. He took a moment to speak, and then all his words came out in an incoherent rush. "I wanted to...but I couldn't...you looked so hot over my knee...didn't want to hurt you...it just felt wrong."

I felt crushed and disappointed. And selfish. After all, I was in the best, most fulfilling relationship I'd ever had, and it still wasn't enough. There was still an itch that needed to be scratched.

"Aren't you going to say something?" The pleading in his voice was clear, but I didn't have any words. Instead, I looked at Matt's face and saw the look of sorrow in his eyes. It was then I realised I wanted to be with him, regardless of whether he spanked me or not. He loved me and I loved him. He understood me, really knew me and had taken me further into my fantasies than I could ever previously have dreamed of.

I leant over and kissed him, a gentle touch of our lips. He kissed back, and it ignited something in us both, a realisation of having being lost and now being found. He rolled on top of me, pressing his mouth down on to mine, pushing his tongue into my mouth. Our teeth clashed in our urgency, his lips bruising as he kissed me harder, emptying my head of every thought except my need for him.

Between us we tugged and pulled at his clothes, and then the duvet, desperate to remove any barrier between us; we become a knot of arms and legs before finally discarding it all on the floor. Matt's cock pushed into my stomach as he lay on top of me, and grew harder still when he pinned me by my wrists, holding me exactly where he wanted me. I writhed impatiently beneath his weight. He kissed and nipped at my lips, my jawline and down my neck. Still holding my wrists tightly, he moved across my collarbone, nuzzling deliciously into the hollows. He darted his tongue at my nipples before taking as much as he could into his mouth, sucking greedily. I couldn't help but wriggle, pushing my hips upwards into his crotch to gain some relief.

"Keep still!" My nipple popped out of his mouth as he admonished me.

"Or what?" I grinned at him, thinking he was too horny to stop what we were doing.

In response, Matt flipped me over, still holding my wrists tightly above my head. I felt his fingers trace round my hairline, and down my spine. His touch was so light, I shivered. He followed up with firmer strokes, digging his fingertips in as he pulled his fingers down my back, ending on my bottom. He pinched and squeezed at my flesh and I couldn't help but wriggle once more.

"You're so desperate to be spanked, aren't you?" His voice was low as I mewled my affirmation at him.

"Please Matt," I found my voice. "Please, let's just try it and see what happens."

He stroked and patted my arse, following its contours with his fingers as he considered. And then he brought his hand down. Not too hard, but enough to surprise me. A mild tingling spread through my cheeks, flooding my senses. I knew that however wet I was before, his one slap had increased it a hundred-fold. As he slapped again, I realised I was holding my breath, savouring the moment.

"How's that?" he asked, as I exhaled slowly.

"More, please, harder." My voice was ragged; heavy with anticipation and fear that he'd stop.

Matt's reply came in gentle pinches and strokes as he examined my flesh. And then he spanked again. And again. Little by little, he soothed and spanked, soothed and spanked. It didn't hurt much, but I was on fire. Something deep in my soul had been ignited and it felt like coming home.

He released my wrists from where he'd been holding them, tight above my head. I reached for his cock, gripping it tightly in my grasp. He was rock solid and I couldn't help feeling relief that he was enjoying this as much as me.

He sat up, leaning against the headboard, propping cushions round his thighs, legs out straight in front of him. I lay still, waiting and wondering. Then Matt pulled me over his knee, my body supported by the mattress. He was rougher this time, as though in his mind, he'd worked out what we both wanted and needed. His cock pressed up hard between my thighs, where he'd positioned me over it and I pushed down to meet it. The pre-come on his head smeared across my clit and I circled my hips, working myself over his hard protrusion, wanting the release from the pressure he'd built inside me.

He had other ideas though, and pulling my wrists into the small of my back, held me there. I couldn't move, not without his say-so. And then he renewed my spanking. This time there was no uncertainty, no hesitation. A few gentle slaps gave way to a rhythmic volley of blows that had my hot, wet and wriggling in no time. Yet, there was still no relief. He spanked like there was no tomorrow, like he was ridding himself of all his doubts.

The pain built and I knew I'd be bruised, little trophies of what we'd done. But I didn't stop him, didn't want to stop him. It felt so right; if ever there was a right kind of pain, this was it. And I wanted him to have a cathartic experience. I needed him to want to do this to me, to want to spank me and not be worried or me to have to badger him into it. Tears formed in my eyes and I knew I could stop it at any moment; all I had to do was say the words. But I didn't want to. I didn't want to be the one to stop this.

I bucked my hips against his thighs at every blow, his cock just nudging into my slick folds. It was torture, feeling so close to climax yet being denied. The heat radiated from my bottom; it had long since suffused though my body, and now my orgasm burned inside of me, roiling and agitating. Every touch of his palm brought me closer. The insistence in my clit was overwhelming and I found myself begging, tears rolling down my face.

"Please Matt, please let me come." I was beside myself, the pleasure and pain combined sent me to a place I'd never been before.

"But I thought you wanted me to spank you?" he teased, stopping his blows to stroke my buttocks. He pinched at the sore, reddened flesh and I winced, not knowing whether I was experiencing ecstasy or pain. "Don't you want me to continue?"

I really didn't know. My head was swimming in an endorphin high, and I didn't know what I wanted. Thankfully, Matt did. He rolled me off his lap and wrapped us both in the duvet, knowing from experience that I was likely to start shivering, despite the warm room. One of the things I loved about him was his attention to my emotional and physical state, knowing exactly what aftercare I needed and when to start administering it.

He also knew how much I needed the release he'd been building inside of me. Holding me tight, he teased my labia apart and slicked his fingers with my wetness. Circling his thumb over my clit, he pushed two fingers inside me and brought me swiftly to climax. It ripped through me, pulsing through my entire body. Somewhere in my brain I registered my buttocks chafing on the bed sheets, and Matt kissing my forehead.

Slowly, I came round. The fog in my mind subsided and I felt able to move. It felt like a huge weight had been lifted; I now knew I was a masochist as well as submissive, and had the bruises to prove it. My thoughts turned to Matt. What about him? Could he cope with this aspect of our relationship?

I reached out and snuggled into his chest, tracing my hands down his back and thighs. Slowly, I arrived round at his cock. It was still hard, coated in pre-cum. He groaned, and I grinned, carrying on from where I'd left off earlier.

"So, did you enjoy spanking me?" I whispered, knowing the answer already.

He groaned again, his abdomen and balls contracting as he orgasmed, coating my stomach in his come.

"I'll take that as a yes then," I grinned and got up to examine my bottom in the mirror.

# BEFORE

She lay in the street, naked and alone. Beads of sweat had gathered on her skin and to any onlooker, she almost shimmered in the post-dawn light. Her mouth was dry, the moisture long absorbed by the grimy cloth stretched tautly between her teeth and tied behind her head. Trying to loosen her aching joints, she moaned; her limbs were still tied.

Slowly wriggling in an attempt to loosen her bonds, yet trying not to scratch her skin on the rough paving, her mind drifted back to what had occurred. She had been out with friends the night before, and on the way home had been in the unfortunate vicinity of one of the gangs. They'd seized her off the street and bundled her into a van, blindfolding, gagging, and tying her so she was unable to either escape or recognise her kidnappers.

Once back at their base, she had been given to their leader. She remembered with a pleasurable yet guilty shiver the touch of his fingers as they'd grazed her flesh, pulling off clothing, and grabbing and pinching wherever they roamed. The feel of his breath on her skin as he focused on his victim. No-one had dared touch her in such a long time and despite the dubious circumstances, her nipples had hardened at his rough touch and the cloying smell of her arousal had left no-one in doubt.

And then it had ended so abruptly. Her kidnappers had not recognised her before their audacious grab and in the light of their warehouse, one of them had realised who she was. They'd quickly dropped her off in Chinatown, fearing for their lives. Wriggling free of her bonds, she idly wondered what to tell her father, the fearsome boss of all the local crime syndicates?

# DIRTY

The doorbell rang and Gilly answered it. Standing on the doorstep was a man that to her was Adonis himself. He stood tall, broad shouldered, hints of muscle where they needed to be, not an ounce of excess fat to be seen. His blue eyes twinkled as he said "I've come to clean your oven." Gilly nearly came at the sound of his voice, smooth and sultry surrounding her senses.

"Can I come in?" he motioned to her, and Gilly jilted herself from her reverie enough to gather her thoughts and stand to the side to let him pass. The heavenly male vision took off his shoes and left them besides the door, before walking through to the kitchen, the location obvious from the front door.

A waft of aftershave hit Gilly's nostrils and she breathed the scent in heavily. She followed him in, watching his tight arse as he walked, and watched as he carefully set down his work bag. Oh, how she longed to run her hands through his hair, scratch her fingertips gently down his naked chest..."Oh, this is dirty."

The man's voice snapped her back to the present. The way he pronounced 'dirty' made her feel, well, filthy. The way he looked at her as he spoke, like she were a mote of dust; she was transfixed by his hypnotic gaze. "I'd better get to work then." He said, his words rippling through Gilly like she was made of jelly. "I'll be as quick as I can."

He seemed to be telling her to leave him to get on with his work. But she didn't want to leave him. She wanted to drink him in, inch by delicious inch. Somehow she found things to do, keeping an eye on him as he bent down to steam and spritz, watching his muscular thighs flex, his forearms bulge then relax. Finally, he stood up and packed his tools away.

"Is there anything else you'd like me to clean?" he asked, his eyes seeming to bore into her very soul, looking as though he knew her mind needed a good soapy scrub. Gilly looked back at him and tried to find the courage, but words failed her. He approached her, looking as though a lion about to devour his prey.

He reached out and picked a small piece of fluff off her shoulder. He looked at it and grimaced. "Dirty...dirty girl..." He reached out and pulled Gilly towards him, until his mouth was level with her ear. He whispered, "I don't think I can make you clean, you're far...too...dirty," into it, and Gilly all but whimpered.

Her breasts were pushing up against his torso; her tight nipples were surely cutting into his chest. And then oh glory, she felt it, the insistent press of his manhood, pushing against her stomach as he held her in place. His eyes met hers and their gazes locked, Gilly hardly dared breathe, not wanting to break the spell. "I need to bathe you," he told her.

Gilly reluctantly moved away from him and taking his hand pulled him upstairs and into the bathroom. The man starting pouring a bath, and as the water level rose, he found a hairbrush and sitting Gilly down, started to gently pull it through her auburn tresses. Once he was satisfied, he deftly tied it up and out of the way of her shoulders, obviously not wanting her to get it wet. Despite still being dressed and just the flesh on the back of her neck exposed, Gilly felt naked and defenceless.

Next, he slowly stripped her. Each item of clothing was folded neatly and placed on the lid of the laundry basket. Despite his height, and large hands he was very gentle as he divested her of her clothes. Every time he came upon a loose thread or a hair, he would hold it up and examine it, muttering "dirty," before disposing of it in the nearby bin.

Finally, the bath was poured and Gilly was naked. "Get in," he commanded, holding her hand in a gentlemanly fashion as she stepped over the side, so as to stop her from losing her balance. Gilly stepped into the warm water and felt cocooned by the bath and the bubbles. The man gently took her hand and started soaping it, slowly moving up her arm; Gilly sighed, his strong soft hands and the relaxation of a bath were delicious.

She was crazy, she knew, letting him clean her as though she were just another job, objectifying her like she was an oven but heck, why not enjoy it? He moved slowly over her body, cleaning her neck, shoulders, even underarms before his hands reached her breasts. His soapy hands slipped and slid over her the delicate skin, her flesh expertly manipulated by his fingertips. They circled her taut nipples, not lingering, just ensuring they got their turn of soap.

Gilly did her best not to moan, feeling so highly erotically charged at this strange and methodical treatment. His hands carried on further down, cleaning her back and belly. Just before he reached her pubic line, he continued down her right leg, stopping slowly to soap each individual toe, before moving back up her left leg. Finally, he had nowhere else to go.

His fingertips traced firmly over her pubic hair, shampooing and massaging. And then, he did the same to her labia, massaging the outsides, before parting them gently to gain access to her inner lips. All the while he maintained a firm yet gently pressure and Gilly felt her own internal pressure rise, knowing that he was bringing her ever closer to climax, but hardly daring to breathe lest she disturb his progress.

At last his fingers found her clitoris and as they worked over the delicate hood, the tingling sensation grew and grew. Gilly moaned and arched herself up into his hand. The man didn't even blink and continued to caress her clitoris as it engorged with blood, whilst his other hand continued to clean between her now-swollen labia, to where her wetness greedily awaited his arrival. He plunged his fingers rhythmically in and out of her, whispering "You're so dirty. You need a good wash. And here...here...is dirtiest of all."

He emphasised 'here' and each time he did so, he plunged his hand ever harder, his fingertips hitting the inside walls of Gilly's vagina, the fingertips of his other hand pushing her hard against her clitoris. Finally, Gilly couldn't fight off the onslaught of her orgasm any longer and she came hard, arching her back up to meeting his hands harder, pulsing against his fingers inside her. He gently withdrew his fingers and stood up, drying his hands on a towel. "It's a good job I left my keys at home isn't it love?"

# BREASTS OR BOTTOM?

We lay lazily on the bed, naked and comfortable, mostly talking, sometimes kissing, and definitely pretending the world didn't exist. We'd gradually moved into a spooning position, and Blair had one arm wrapped under me whilst his free hand was running tantalisingly slowly up and down my torso.

"Do you prefer my breasts or my bottom?" I enquired, out of idle curiosity.

"What sort of question is that?" he laughed at me. "Of course I like both!"

"No, pick one!" I told him insistently, grabbing his hand to stop him from touching me until he'd answered.

He wiggled his fingers out of my tight grasp and they gravitated towards my nipples. "If I had to choose I'd have to say breasts," he said seriously. "I love your bottom, but I love your breasts more."

His fingers circled my nipples and tweaked them as they got harder, making me gasp with pleasure tinged with a hint of pain. He pulled me back into him with his muscular arms and I felt him hardening against me, his cock pressing ever more insistently into the back of my thighs. Meanwhile his fingers continued to graze my nipples, alternately pinching and caressing. He cupped my breasts one at a time, squeezing first gently then harder, and making me moan with pleasure. I was getting more turned on by the minute, and pushed my bottom back into his crotch, feeling his hard cock pressing back in return.

Suddenly, I was lying on my back, Blair straddling me. He nuzzled my neck with his lips, barely touching my skin, then kissed insistently whilst moving downwards, towards my breasts. He buried his face there, before licking and sucking at my nipples, one at a time, using his fingers to tweak and tease the one not in his mouth. "Yes," he murmured distractedly. "Definitely your breasts. They're definitely your sexiest asset."

He rolled over and slipped on a condom, before pulling me on top. Straddling him, I lowered myself onto his hard cock, sitting upright whilst he played with my breasts; he cupped them in his hands, kneading my flesh as I moved up and down. I lowered my face to kiss him but instead of meeting my lips, he took my right nipple into his mouth, sucking and nibbling. I groaned with pleasure and threw my head back, grinding my hips harder against him. He answered by rolling my left nipple between his fingertips.

We fell into a rhythm, him playing with my breasts whilst I moved up and down against him. As I reached my climax, he tweaked my nipples harder, knowing how my nipples hotline to my pussy, to make me orgasm harder. I pulsed strongly around his cock as the pleasure hit me, and it pushed him over the edge too, his hips bucking up to meet mine for his final few thrusts.

Afterwards, we lay there again, his free hand stroking up and down my body and coming to rest on my bottom.

"You know Ali," he whispered conspiratorially, "I may have got that wrong." He gave my bottom a playful slap. "Perhaps I need to re-acquaint myself with your very fine ass!"

# ROOM SERVICE

"What took you so long? I called for room service an hour ago." I stood in the open doorway. A shiver ran through me, clad as I was in just my underwear.

"I'm sorry." The waiter was terse; he obviously didn't mean it.

"Well, you'd best come in," I stepped back to let him over the threshold.

He pushed past me. I sighed, this was not a great level of customer service.

Taking a deep breath, I closed the door and turned to face the usurper. Anger flashed from my eyes, and I saw him take a step back as he noticed.

"What on earth makes you think I will tolerate rudeness or pushing?" My voice was sharp. A thrilling shiver ran through me. I so enjoyed toying with these weak men.

"I'm sorry ma'am." At least he had the sense to give me the right reply, in the right tone.

"Now, the customer is always right, yes?" I reached into my travel case and pulled out a riding crop. Slapping it down hard into my palm, I had the pleasure of seeing him wince. "Now, you have a choice. You can either leave now, and I will be delighted to let your employer know of your behaviour. Or you can bend over the desk, take your trousers down and I will punish you."

I watched his expressions as the consequences of each choice ran over his face. I knew what he'd choose. At least behind closed doors, his silly male pride wouldn't entirely be in tatters. Private humiliation would always be better than public.

He walked over to the desk, unfastening his belt to let his trousers pool at his ankles, and positioned himself over it. I followed, and used the tip of the crop to widen his legs a little. He winced as it touched, and I smiled. I didn't need to change his position, but it made for good psychological effect.

"Reach your arms out so you are holding on to the far edge of the table." I barked my command. "Now, I want you to count, and thank me for each stroke." He didn't know that I was ogling his bottom through his tight briefs, no point in stroking his precious ego.

He was breathing faster, steeling himself for what was to come. I raised my arm and let the crop fall onto his right buttock. My crop makes a wonderful noise, the swish as it moves through the air, then the crack as it lands. But it's definitely more bark than bite. Again, a little psychological trifling that I enjoy, and doesn't really do any harm, just adds to the effect.

"One, ma'am. Thank you."

Swish and crack on the other buttock.

"Two, ma'am. Thank you."

I ramped up the force, he seemed to be taking it well. By ten he was breathing heavily, it was obviously starting to hurt.

I took him to twenty. After all, he had to learn.

"Get up." I watched as he pulled up his trousers and tried to buckle his belt, fingers fumbling.

"Now, have you learnt your lesson?" I asked.

"Yes ma'am. Thank you, ma'am." He replied, looking down at his feet.

"Good. You did well, baby." I kissed Mark hard on the mouth, letting him know that playtime was over. We were well suited. I like playing the mean bitch; he loved being at my mercy.

"Do I get a tip?" he asked, a cheeky grin on his face.

"Yeah, don't give me any lip, or it'll be the riding crop for you again," I replied, smiling.

# SEPARATION

I'd always wanted to time travel, ever since I was a little girl. I guess it was the same in the twentieth century, when people dreamt of following Neil Armstrong to the moon, hundreds of years ago.

So when I was offered a place on the Human History Project, I jumped at the chance: "An opportunity to catalogue the true events of our history to help us move forwards in the twenty-fifth century."

The premise was simple – we would each be assigned an era that matched our interests and specialities, then we could zap back and forth as needed, to verify the information we already held, and add to it as necessary.

We'd have to travel in what we affectionately called "bubble wrap"; a fool proof way of not interacting with the past, that also rendered us invisible to whoever was there. That was the theory.

I'd been working on 1970's London when I met him. He was tall and lithe, with piercings and cropped hair. I was fascinated; modern-day folk are nothing like he was. I watched him masturbate; I was a voyeur. He was raw and uninhibited, grunting as he pumped his cock like there was no tomorrow. When he came, creamy liquid spilling over his hands, he opened his eyes and looked straight into mine.

I don't know who was more startled. How could he see me? I watched, horrified, fascinated, as his spunky fingers reached me, hitting the side of my protective layer. His eyes were a green, bright green, his post-orgasmic haze quickly lifting.

I wanted to feel him, I really did, but knew it was impossible. I lifted my fingers to match his. And there we stayed, me suspended in my bubble, him reaching up as though I were an angel, fingertips together, with a barrier of time and space between.

I went back to see him as often as I could. We couldn't physically connect or talk, but we were somehow connected. And then one day he wasn't there. A tear rolled down my face as I heard how he'd been locked in the mental hospital. He told everyone who'd listened of an angel who appeared in a bubble, over his bed. But no-one believed him.

I never time-travelled again.

# AN ALFRESCO SPANKING

Shellie and Jim had been hiking for about an hour when they reached the clearing. They'd seen no one since they'd joined the trail. On this beautiful sunny day, it seemed it was just them and the birds in the world.

The clearing was small but awash with sunlight. In the middle, there was a fallen tree trunk. "Perfect," said Jim. "Shellie, it's time." He took off his rucksack and walked over to the trunk, sitting down and making himself comfortable.

Shellie meanwhile was still a bit aghast at what was about to happen. Of course, that's the problem with sharing your fantasies, they might come true. She'd wanted to know what it was like to have her bare bottom spanked in the fresh air, helplessly over someone's knee, but this..? Now it was becoming a reality, it was suddenly too much!

Jim knew Shellie was struggling with her thoughts and decided to take her in hand. If her fantasies were about to be realised, and he had agreed to do this for her, he had to make sure it happened. "Get over here now!" He insisted, decisively.

Shellie hesitated just one more second before going to stand in front of Jim. "Take off your trousers, and get over my knee," he firmly commanded. "Yes Jim." Shellie breathed softly as she did as she was told.

Once positioned, Shellie realised that there was no way back. The slight slope in front of the trunk meant that whilst Jim's feet were firmly on the ground, her petit frame meant there was no way she was going to get any purchase. She was totally suspended across Jim's thighs and at his mercy.

Jim started off slowly and gently, getting Shellie used to the feel of his palm against her buttocks. Very rhythmically, he alternated between her cheeks, building up his strokes so they were harder and faster. As she'd shamefacedly requested that he would be stern and punish her, he only struck the fleshy middle, over and over, to make her really feel the spanking. The noise echoed around the clearing, louder and louder.

Shellie began to squirm, the feeling building up in her bottom was getting more and more painful. He kept on hitting the same damn spot each time, not letting the feeling dissipate before he spanked her again.

"Keep still, Shellie, or you'll only make it worse for yourself," Jim admonished her. He landed his next blow perfectly, knowing that she couldn't help herself but wriggle. "I warned you!"

Jim started peeling Shellie's panties down. Shellie's face flamed red with embarrassment. Jim couldn't see it, he was marvelling at her reddening bottom, his spanking evident against her soft, pale skin.

He started spanking again, and Shellie moaned. This was so much worse! Somehow, the thin layer of fabric of her panties had protected her from the harshness of his blows. Spank, spank, spank, spank! "Is this what you want, Shellie?" Jim asked, "Is this what you needed, someone to take you in hand?"

"Y...ye...yes, Jim," Shellie stuttered out a reply, as tears started to form. She never realised that it would feel like this! She felt so vulnerable, let alone feeling the pain of his blows and the softness of the breeze around her naked buttocks and thighs.

Spank, spank, spank! SPANK, SPANK, SPANK! Jim's blows were relentless and soon, tears were rolling down Shellie's face. As soon as Jim realised Shellie was crying, he decided she'd had a sufficient spanking for her first one. "Right, Shellie, that's enough I think." Jim helped her back to her feet, holding her for balance as she pulled her panties back up.

"Thank you, Jim," Shellie's eyes were bright and she was smiling. Jim picked up his rucksack, and they walked back down the trail together, his hand and Shellie's bottom still stinging.

# STRANGER IN TOWN

The town was Cool, in both name and climate. Not too hot and not too cold. In fact, it should have been named "average", as nothing ever happened. Curtains twitched of course but the most exciting game was "keeping up with the Jones's", as Sarah so cynically described her boring life.

She was a waitress in the local café. It was all decked out to look like a Western saloon, full of cliché but little else. Until one afternoon that was, when a stranger literally rode into town.

Sarah heard the roar of the motor well before the chromed hog came into view. Atop was straddled a leather-clad god. He swung his leg back over the saddle and planted both feet firmly on the ground. Sarah could feel the disapproval radiating through the town, even as she admired the tall stranger.

He pulled off his helmet to show tousled dark curls falling to his shoulders, piercing blue eyes and a week's worth of stubble. Sarah felt her insides melting as she contemplated the vision before her. A jolt ran through her body as their eyes locked; it engorged her nipples and connected through her belly to her now impatiently waiting clit.

The pent-up frustration of 20 years of living in Cool was finally unbearable. And the stranger seemed to know. He wandered into the café, letting the saloon doors swing in his wake. Turning to look at Sarah, he raised one eyebrow and she followed him in.

He beckoned to Sarah to come closer and she did. Standing before him, so unsure of herself in comparison with him, she felt him undressing her with his eyes. She breathed in deeply, and tried to calm her fluttering pulse.

He grabbed her wrist and pulled her close, sliding his other hand round to the nape of her neck. Sarah felt owned, excited and was dripping with lust. She leant in to allow him access to her mouth, allowing her instincts to take over. Their lips met, a wild mashing of lips and teeth; Sarah realised she was done with ordinary romance, she wanted adventure!

The newcomer tasted exotic to Sarah, she savoured his sweat and musk. As he hurriedly unzipped his jacket, large, tight muscles emerged, framed by a t-shirt that was a size too small. Sarah couldn't keep her hands off him, running her hands down his chest, teasing her nails down his biceps.

And then he was propelling her backwards into the ladies' bathroom. Backed up against the cold tiles, she gasped as his fingers roughly tugged her nipples through her blouse, and more as he leant into her, his big thigh pressing heavily against her mons.

"I don't even know your name," Sarah feebly tried to object to his touch, wishing fervently for more. In return, he pressed two calloused fingers hard against her mouth before replacing them with his lips, his stubble scratching at her chin.

Sarah reached for his fly, and pulling the zip down hard, allowed his cock to spring loose. It was hard, angry-looking, its shaft marbled with veins. And big, so big, Sarah thought, getting wetter as she thought about him impaling her. She pumped her hand up and down the shaft and he growled in approval, moving his lips from hers roughly down her exposed neck.

"You're a delicious little thing," he snarled, holding her hair to one side to access her skin better. "I want to eat you all up."

A shiver ran through Sarah as she realised she was at the mercy of this stranger, this man who'd mesmerised her. It just added to her excitement and she felt herself getting moister as she worked his cock.

He worked his hand up her skirt and roughly pulling her panties to one side, rolled his forefinger over her plump clitoris. Sarah nearly came at his coarse touch. "Please," she croaked, unable to contain herself any longer.

The stranger laughed throatily. "All in good time, girl," and continued to explore her body. He plunged two fingers easily inside her, sliding them back and forth, coated in her wetness. His other hand slid under her blouse, finding and tweaking her nipples, pinch, pull, pinch, pull.

Sarah found herself floating into a state of ecstatic bliss, on the brink of orgasm; her whole body was shaking and aching for release. The stranger was murmuring in her ear, encouraging her climax, telling her to scream and let it all out. His words aren't making sense, Sarah dimly thought, but her primal instincts had kicked in; her body was primed for climax, not thought. "You smell so good, c'mon girl, release those endorphins, I want my fix," he coaxed, insistently.

The world seemed to fall away from Sarah as her orgasm rushed upon her in violent waves, sending spasms through her whole body. As each new muscular contraction gripped the fingers now still inside her, she realised that it hurt, her neck fucking hurt. Everything dimmed and seemed to be running in slow motion as she screamed, obedient to the stranger's last word. Her lifeless body fell to the blood-spattered floor.

# BUTTERFLY

I was tired and angry as we arrived at the hotel. We had picked up the wrong fucking suitcase. What I wanted was my own pyjamas and a good night's sleep; what I got was frustration from trying to talk to the airline's customer service department.

I was in the bathroom, attempting to clean my teeth with toothpaste squeezed onto my index finger, when Jay called through. "Hey, baby, you should see what I've found in the case!" There was excitement in his voice. Despite myself, I wondered what he'd found. It had been a long time since I'd last heard him sound animated by anything, including me.

I wandered lazily back through to the bedroom and saw Jay carefully holding up a corset. It was stunning. Purple silk, black lace, diamantes.

"Try it on," Jay urged, not that I needed encouragement. He loosened off the lacing at the back, fingers working methodically as he kept the tension even.

I was naked, him fully dressed, both of us now aroused. I held the silk-boned panels in place as he knelt in front of me, fastening the clasps, each one moulding the corset closer to my skin. Jay stood up, and turned me to face the mirror. I watched, fascinated, my new shape emerging as he systematically tightening the lacing.

The corset gripped tighter and each tug on the lace made me gasp; being cinched in was an exquisite torture that I never wanted to end. Finally Jay finished and he stood behind me, our eyes locked in the mirror. We both looked at me, but it wasn't me. It was a mirage that didn't feel real as he ran his hands over my sculpted flesh. He gripped at my thighs, thrusting his cock harder against the furrow of my buttocks. Excitement shone in his eyes; a wild look emerged. I hadn't seen it before, but then I hadn't seen me look like this before.

He spanked my arse, hard, just once in exploration and I squirmed, trapped between the table and his thighs. It stung, but hell, I wanted it! Wiggling my bottom as best I could, I goaded him into more. He slapped my bottom until it glowed red hot; I squealed, he slapped harder.

"Is this what you want?" he hissed at me, his arousal evident in his every word, every movement.

"Yes," I cried, not knowing what it was I wanted, but knew it was this.

His fingertips dug in my thigh and I felt him reaching for something. A condom. I watched in the mirror as he tore open the pack with his teeth, and still gripping me, unfastened his trousers and rolled on the rubber sheath one-handed. He released my thigh and skimmed his hand over the top of my breasts, their flesh rounded and tight in the corset. His hand moved up my throat; I whimpered. Finally, he brushed his fingertips over my lips as though contemplating his next move.

Roughly he pushed two fingers into my mouth, and his cock into my wet, needy hole. There was no gentleness, just sheer animalistic rutting. His fingers hooked behind my teeth, anchoring me; I couldn't move if I tried. His other hand worked forcefully down the cleft between my legs, probing, prising. He pinched and pulled at my labia. It should have hurt but it only made me wetter.

I floated towards ecstasy and thought of myself as a butterfly pinned to a board. Probed and used, until the novelty wore off, bright colours fading.

# CONFERENCE

Julia stifled a yawn. The conference was dull, immeasurably so. The joint speakers were under-rehearsed both with each other, the presentation material and one of them could barely be heard, through lack of volume after the microphone broke. She shifted uncomfortably in her seat, her back and legs feeling cramped in her allocated space.

As she moved, her skirt rode a fraction up her legs and out of the corner of her eye she realised her colleague Richard had also moved. His gaze settled on her knees and moved up appreciatively to where her skirt now sat. Julia and Richard had flirted reciprocally on occasion but it was mainly office banter, or after a few drinks when letting off steam after yet another interminably dull conference day. Once or twice they had made it into a hotel room together where they had shared more than a drink.

Richard's gaze moved back to the speakers and he appeared to be making a few notes. He tapped his finger a few times where he had written to get Julia's attention and she glanced over to read "This is dull. Fancy some fun?" She raised an eyebrow questioningly at him and he wrote something new down. "The things I want to do to you but I can't right now. So you'll have to do them to yourself."

Again Julia looked questioningly at him but Richard smiled a wry grin and his eyes twinkled as he wrote. "Hitch your skirt a little higher so I can see your sexy legs." Julia felt her cheeks flush but at the same time there was a flutter of excitement in her belly. What would he have her do?

"I see you've accepted my challenge," his scribbling continued, "your first task is to give me your panties." Julia was a little shocked. Sure Richard was a nice guy but he wasn't usually this forward. He tapped his pen impatiently. Julia checked to see that no one was looking and through her skirt found the waistband of her thong and started working it surreptitiously down.

She couldn't help but notice a growing bulge at Richard's crotch. He noticed too and quickly pulled his conference pack back to cover his growing excitement. Julia shifted in her seat again but this time to lift her hips to slide her thong underneath them. Her conference pack, opened up on her knee, was ample camouflage for her clandestine activities, and she smiled to herself as she felt them drop round her ankles.

After carefully stepping out of them, she reached down and bunched them up into her hand. Richard took them from her, and just like they were a hanky, wiped them across his face, inhaling Julia's scent. He quickly dropped them into his pocket, looking to enjoy Julia's shocked look followed by her blushing, as she realised have he had smelt her wetness and knew just how turned on she was by their naughty game.

Julia waited for his next instruction and didn't have to wait long. "Show me more of your luscious thighs." Julia hitched her skirt up more, wondering how far she dared go. Her pussy involuntarily clenched at the embarrassing thought of exposing herself, or leaving a damp patch on the seat.

"I know you're turned on. Taste yourself." Julia nearly audibly groaned, how on earth was she going to do that without being spotted? She knew how wet she was, how shockingly turned on by this out of character behaviour for them both. She couldn't do it, just couldn't and shook her head. A doodle of a chicken appeared on Richard's notes and despite herself, Julia smiled.

Then she saw his next note "Finish playing this game and you'll get a whole night of unadulterated pleasure from me." Again, Julia nearly groaned. Richard was great in bed. An attentive lover whose kisses and caresses alone she would die for, let alone the feel of his thick shaft plunging in and out of her, or his tongue lacking expertly at her clit until she came.

Pulling her conference pack up over her thighs and leaning forward slightly so her suit jacket obscured the view, Julia worked her hand under the waistband of her skirt. Her nakedness beneath her hand, flesh when there should have been fabric, sent a thrill through her sex, fuelling the fire building there.

Pushing her hand further down, she parted her fleshy lips, grazing her fingertips over her clit, and rapidly pushed two fingers inside. She felt her nipples harden as she did so and caught her breath at the heady rush of sensations. A tap of a pen brought Julia's attention back to the room and slipping her hand back out of her skirt, she turned to Richard and looking him right in the eye, pushed her glistening fingers into her mouth and sucked them clean, sliding them in and out of her lips. She was rewarded by the wide eyed look on Richard's face and saw by the rise and fall of his shoulders that he was currently feeling as horny she was.

Grabbing his pen he quickly scribbled "Fuck I want you!" but before he had chance to continue writing, the sound of a light smattering of applause interrupted. Julia smiled - they were in different breakout sessions for the rest of the day so the promised night of passion was hers.

# ANNABELLE GOT SPANKED

"In your school uniform now!" Annabelle jumped at the sound of Stephan's voice and gasped. She hadn't expected him to be back so soon, and was lounging around in her jeans, listening to music, after finishing work for the day. She'd completely forgotten that they'd agreed to play "schoolgirl" that night.

"I expect to see you downstairs in five minutes." And with that, he had turned on his heel and was gone.

Annabelle took a deep breath and quickly slipped her jeans and t-shirt off, hurriedly put on her white blouse, and slid her school dress over her head. It was short, barely reaching mid-thigh length. She wondered what she could do to help her redeem herself, and decided that some nice, silky stockings might work. She took off her panties, put on the stockings, and put her panties back on over the top, pleased with her quick thinking.

She checked her appearance in the mirror, and not without some trepidation, went downstairs. Stephan was sitting on one of the high-backed chairs with no arms and Annabelle gulped, realising that a spanking was likely. She stood demurely, her hands clasped behind her back, her eyes downcast.

Somehow though, she managed to knock his pen off the table next to her and sent it clattering to the floor. "Pick that up!" Stephan commanded her, irritation in his voice. She turned around and picked up the pen, giving him a full view of the tops of her stockings and her tiny lacy black panties.

As she straightened up, she felt him behind her. "What's this, Annabelle, stockings?" His hands moved up and down her thighs and buttocks. "And your panties are barely there. You really do have some bare-face cheek!"

She managed a wry smile at his joke, but he was on it in a flash. "This is no laughing matter, young lady. Inappropriate underwear with your uniform. Your uniform incidentally, that you weren't wearing when I came home. That deserves punishment. Over my knee!"

Annabelle found herself being dragged over to the seat and Stephan settled himself down, with his knees wide apart, ready to receive her weight across them. She knew the drill and grimaced as he positioned her better, pulling her by the waist here, pulling her right leg there. It was part of the ritual of him getting ready to spank her, taking his time with her like that, like psychological warfare.

He pulled her skirt right up, and his first spank landed hard on her right butt cheek. "Ow," she whimpered as she felt the smart emanating from his palm. He were obviously mad at her, as there was no gentle warm up. The next blow landed, then the next. The stings spread and built, and Annabelle wriggled, but there was no escape. She felt his cock stiffening, constrained by his trousers. The bulge pressed into her thigh, and she pressed back against it, hoping it would distract him from his task. However, he didn't seem to notice and continued landing blow after blow.

Stephan knew her well enough to understand that after a few minutes of treatment like that, the endorphins would kick in and she wouldn't feel the spanking as hard as he wanted her to, so he upped the pressure, spanking her even harder.

"Please," she begged, "I'm sorry for not being in my uniform. I'm really sorry."

"Tell me how much you're sorry," his voice was

stern, and she gulped.

"Please stop spanking me sir, I'll do anything you want." The blows were so hard, she just wanted them to stop and at that point, she would do anything.

"Hmmm, anything," Stephan mused, as he continued to spank her. she felt his hand slip under her panties and round to her wet pussy. She shivered, feeling naked and vulnerable as he slipped first one, then two fingers inside her. "Oh Annabelle, you're such a little slut aren't you? Getting so wet, even as I'm punishing you!"

She let out a sob, knowing that he was right. "Stand up!" He commanded, helping her to her feet.

"So, you promised me anything in return for me to stop spanking you. Anything is a dangerous game, young lady, I hope you thought this through." He unzipped his trousers and his huge, hard cock sprang out towards her. He fisted his fingers into the back of her hair and pushed her down to her knees in front of himself, guiding her mouth insistently towards his awaiting shaft.

She had no choice but to wrap her lips around his head, already moist with pre-cum. Stephan held her head tight and very slowly pushed his cock into her mouth, then pulled out again. She tried to relax her jaw, knowing he would fuck her mouth for as long as he wanted. She brought up her hands, and stroked his balls, and along the base of his shaft. She knew there was a risk he would punish her further, for using her hands without permission like that, but she also knew the extra stimulation would drive him wild. He moaned, then realised what she was doing, and using her hair like reins, pulled her back to her feet.

"You really are pushing it this time, young lady." He growled at her, and Annabelle wondered what would happen next. He pulled her back upstairs, his hand still in her hair, and when they were in the bedroom, he took off his trousers and pants. Stephan laid back on the bed, with his hands behind his head, looking for all the world relaxed, and a man about to receive what he wanted all along. Anna started to remove her panties but was told to leave them on.

She straddled Stephan, and pushing her panties to the side, lowered herself onto his cock a bit at a time, feeling her juices lubricate his shaft and allowing her pussy to adjust to his girth. She slid herself up and down his cock, feeling his tension build. He moaned, and reached his hands round to her butt, holding on to her just-spanked cheeks to steer himself towards his inevitable climax.

He pulled and pushed her up and down his shaft until she felt his stomach muscles contract, telling her that his orgasm was close. She clenched and relaxed her muscles against his cock, knowing how much he liked it. Again and again he manipulated her until he tensed up, then relaxed and she felt him spurting his come into her, warm, sticky and wet.

She moved off him, and Stephan pulled her down beside himself, holding her tightly. "I love you," he whispered to her, "and I think you should get a reward for taking your punishment so well."

His hand moved down between her thighs, and she turned onto her back, opening her legs wide to allow him access, as he expertly handled her clit. He stroked, and pinched and rubbed until she was arching her back, desperate for the release that his fingers were promising. "Are you a good girl, Annabelle?" he asked.

"Yes," she cried back at him, "Yes I am a good girl. Please let me come."

"Tell me why, Annabelle," he teased her, knowing how desperate this would wind her up.

"Because I take my punishment so well. Please let me come, please..." With that, Stephan murmured "yes" in her ear and deftly stroked her engorged clitoris, getting the timing and pressure just right. She arched her back, pushing herself down onto his fingers, her body shuddering as the orgasm hit, wave after wave.

"I love you baby." she told him later, when he pulled her close, and stroked her hair, letting her come down slowly from the intensity of what they'd just done. "I'll always be your naughty school girl.".

# 100 WORDS: A BONUS FEATURE

*As a writing challenge, I wrote a series of first-person vignettes limited to exactly 100 words each. I admit I cheated on the last one – it's actually 200 words, but it insisted on being told in its own way!*

\*\*\*

I lay quivering at his touch. His fingers insistently stroking the mound of flesh just above my clit from north to south. Over and over, driving me wilder with want, need, desire. The slightest caress causing pleasure to ripple through me, edging me ever closer to that elusive orgasm. My back arched towards him as far as my bonds allowed; a mewl escaped my lips as I tried to obey his command not to come. Over and over he pressed his fingertips to my flesh, filling my mind with longing for release and lust for him, him and only him.

\*\*\*

The first spank was a warning to prepare me for what was to come, rather than an assault on my bare bottom. It was a gentle tap followed by a circling of his palm over my left cheek, then leisurely repeated on my right. Tap, rub, tap rub, tap, rub, he formed an easy rhythm. The stroke of his hand slowly worked its way up in intensity, the tempo incrementally increasing until the short sharp sting of his hand made my bottom sing with a pink glow of pleasure. Each pulse of an emerging rhythm expertly conducted by his hand.

\*\*\*

Oh, his kiss. His powerful, erotically charged kiss. The one that simultaneously takes my breath away whilst making me go weak at the knees. He strokes his fingers down my cheek, run his fingertips along my jawline and gently hooks my chin up so I am forced to look into his big, brown, sexy, come-to-bed eyes. Ever so slowly, he lowers his lips to lightly graze mine, barely brushing them, leaving me wanting more. His kisses are so soft, his touch so delicate, so addictive, that I want him, no need him to continue to press his mouth to mine.

\*\*\*

When I thought I couldn't take any more of his teasing, he'd slide his hand behind my head, twisting his fingers firmly into my hair at my nape, so there was no escape and he'd press his lips insistently to my own, me opening my mouth to his by instinct, allowing his tongue to roam my mouth. He'd push it in so deep that it would force my mouth open further, and I would be truly helpless before him. He'd consume me, ravage me, leave me breathless, panting, feeling owned, turned on, so erotically charged, so wanted, so needed, his.

\*\*\*

He'd take both my wrists in one hand and hold me helpless, unable to move. His other hand would roam up and down my torso, stroking, caressing, grabbing. I'd moan and let him do whatever he wanted. He'd pinch and grab at my buttocks, pulling me into him, so I could feel the growing bulge at his crotch. He'd work his fingers into my bra, squeezing my breasts, pinching my nipples; his breath hot and ragged against my neck as he whispered, "You like that, don't you, baby?" to me. All I could do in reply was nod and whimper.

\*\*\*

The thought of being spanked was something that sparked in my head but got pushed to the dusty unloved corners of my imagination, knowing it would never be fulfilled and therefore was to be ignored.

Until the day he spanked me for the first time, when I asked him to put me over his knee. When he doesn't spank me regularly now, I miss the pain; miss the release. Then I beg him to spank me; I think he enjoys the begging nearly as much as the act itself, knowing that he can give me what I want, need, crave.

\*\*\*

Had I had a choice but to submit to his will, my head and heart holding me hostage to it? Always. But I was enthralled, enrapt, my heart held captive by his, what we did together and the bond we shared. My willing submission was a gift I happily gave and he took my gift with the gratitude of someone who knew what it truly meant. And he nurtured this gift; my moans and groans as he inflicted torment and torture, pleasure and pain, on my eager, sometimes traitorous body, always pushing my boundaries, never going further than we agreed.

\*\*\*

My arms were stretched so my hands could hold onto the table edges. My face was pressed against the unyielding wooden surface, the blindfold shaped to the contours of my cheeks cutting out any light. I was reliant on my other senses, straining to hear the slightest noise. I was bent over at my waist; my ankles, tied to the table legs, had been pushed apart by his thigh pressing insistently between my legs, his hands persuading, no bending, my body to his will. I was his captive, unable to go anywhere; my body was entirely his, for his enjoyment.

\*\*\*

Your fingers trail down my torso, over my breasts, across the delicate skin of my stomach; skim across my inner thighs. Up and round again. Circling ever closer, but not touching my sweet core, with its power to unlock my sexuality and permit my femininity to burst forward, drowning us both in a tidal wave of desire. Allowing me to lose my inhibitions, show who I truly am in those precious moments building up to climax. Then we see who you are as you take me over that peak and into the beyond, holding me close as the waves subside.

\*\*\*

I am your slut, sir, your whore.  Right now, I'm a horny bitch for you. I will crawl to you, beg you. Let you plunder the depths of my depravity and take me to places within that I don't even know exist, sir. I am yours for the taking, sir, for your pleasure. I am your toy to fuck, to touch, to pleasure, to torment.  Please bind me, blindfold me, silence me, spank me, use clamps on me. Flog me, use the riding crop on me, make me scream your name in pleasure and pain. I am your slut, sir.

\*\*\*

I waited now, waited for him to touch me. Perhaps he would caress me, so gently, so lovingly. His fingertips would graze smoothly over my skin, firing off every neuron as they made contact, inch by inch, making me shiver in anticipation. Perhaps he would massage, pinch and roll my flesh, digging in his nails, making me moan for more and arch my body into him. Or perhaps he would spank me, turning the flesh of my bottom red with application of his palm to my behind. which my body would translate into a spreading glow of warmth and euphoria.

\*\*\*

"You're mine!" you growl as you grab me by my arm and propel me to the wall. There I am pinned by your body pressed into mine, your cock hard against my stomach as you push your mouth impatiently on to mine, wanting me as much as I want you. You fist one hand into my hair, as your lips roam, their insistent pressure on my cheek, my neck, my collarbone, and your stubble grazing across my skin. Your other hand roughly grabs my waist, my breasts, my buttocks, pulling me in 1000 different directions, yet ever closer to you.

***

You crawl across the bed, slowly stalking me on all fours. The light behind you silhouettes your form and catches your outline, making you appear to glow, as I lay here unable to move. The glint in your eye is hungry, predatory, and captured here as I am, I feel like prey, helpless and vulnerable. I see your biceps tighten and relax as you move closer to me and am reminded of your physical strength. The power you have to be gentle and soothing, or rough and exciting. The physical power to match your mental prowess when playing with me.

***

I want you to bind my limbs so I'm helpless, gag me into silence, have me lie next to you as you read. Have me feel helpless and utterly yours as you absentmindedly stroke my hair or run your finger down my cheek and along my jawbone. Have me wait for you, until you are ready and tell me that I've been a good girl. Or make me wait because you can. I want you to whisper naughtiness in my ear and if I wriggle or make too much noise, I want you to punish me, make me feel owned.

***

I want to feel your masculinity engulf me. Feel your manliness swamp my every sense; enclose me in our own secluded space. The essence of you to fill my nostrils. The noise of you, your whispers and commands to envelope my ears. The sight of your manhood to make me needy, the thought of it inside me to make me wet with desire. I want to feel sweaty and sated with you; your hard insistent throbbing to overcome my soft yielding flesh, my delicate touch. The taste of you, salty, tangy, sweet and sour, I want it on my tongue.

***

"You'd better come, bitch, to show me how much you appreciate what I do to you," you said as you pumped your hips harder into mine, stamping your presence and ownership on every cell that you make contact with. But I wonder how I am ever going to, being so overwhelmed with sensation. Until then I'd just been enjoying the ride, and now you've put the pressure on. My bindings make it hard to find that oh-so-right position and your insistent thrusts aren't in quite the right place. But I know I have to, to please you, to obey you.

***

Our bodies press together and I feel totally relaxed in your arms. Heat radiates from you and I lap it up, pushing myself closer for more. My breasts are crushed against your chest, and you hold me in place. One arm is around my shoulders, pulling me tighter; the other stroking and fondling my back, bottom and thighs. I can't help but purr like a kitten; I am putty in your knowing hands. Your hard cock radiates the most heat and I repeatedly push my hips against it until you push me onto my back and make love to me.

***

"Look at me," you command as I lower my eyes from your gaze, to stop you from seeing the truth. It hurts more for me to know that you can see how much I relish the pain, than the pain itself. You hold my chin up to force me to meet your scrutiny as you spank my breasts. I flinch from the sensation yet devour the pain. Meanwhile I can't look away from you as you see the pleasure in my eyes, and in return I see my true self reflected back at me, and know I'm forever your slut.

***

You seem to know me better than I know myself. You know when I need you to make love to me, or when I need to be fucked. It's like you're hardwired into my brain, able to make sense of the chaos that I let loose inside my head. You take charge of it, forming order from my disarray. Take charge of my body, setting me free from my insecurities and self-doubts. You accept me for who I am and love and worship every inch of me inside and out, despite myself. And I love and worship you in return.

***

Pulled roughly over a pile of pillows on the bed, I nervously wait for your next move. I know you will punish me, but for what transgression, and what will my behaviour warrant? The cane, the crop, the paddle or your palm? I feel the warmth in your hand from the first strike but the more you spank, the less I feel your hand until I am liquid fire, a whirling pool of pleasure and pain, tears and euphoria. You swap instruments to torture my buttocks some more but I am oblivious to the individual strikes, my submission completely yours.

***

As he fucks me, I lie pinned beneath him. My hands are grasped tightly in his, my legs pushed wide apart by his own. The sweat we've generated glazes us together, smoothing away the friction as his hips thrust up into me, spearing me on his cock. His breath runs more ragged now and I feel his ferocity as he drives harder, deeper, urging ever forward for his release. I feel myself tightening around him, wanting him to gain that pleasure from using my body, feeling his tension coiling. His urgency increases, his thrusting ever deeper until victory is his.

\*\*\*

I stand as instructed with my legs far apart. You have my wrists pinned together, anchored by your hand in the small of my back. Partly for stability and to hold me in place, partly to remind me of your dominance over me and finally as a reminder that I willingly submit to this. I feel your hand strike at the delicate flesh between my legs; feel the sharp sting as my clit absorbs the impact. It brings tears to my eyes and I involuntarily take a quick breath, to try and numb the pain. You rub gently over my pubic mound and clit with your fingertips to take the sting away, and I try to press myself into your hand for the pleasurable relief. You whisper "naughty!" into my ear and strike me again. You repeat the torment and pleasure cycle over and over until I'm not sure what I want more. The heady sensation of pleasure alternated with pain, the hurt-so-bad contrasting with the hurt-so-good, your soothing strokes mixed with your stinging blows, it's too much to take in. You have turned me into a quivering begging heap of lust and submission, and the night has barely begun.

## ONE LAST THING...

**If you enjoyed this book** I'd really appreciate if you would post a short review on Amazon. Your support really does make a difference and I read all the reviews personally so I can get your feedback and improve my writing.

**If you didn't like it**, please visit my website at iamannasky.com and send me an email to let me know why.

Thanks again for your support!

9759672R00048

Printed in Great Britain
by Amazon.co.uk, Ltd.,
Marston Gate.